Just one more thing ...and then bedtime

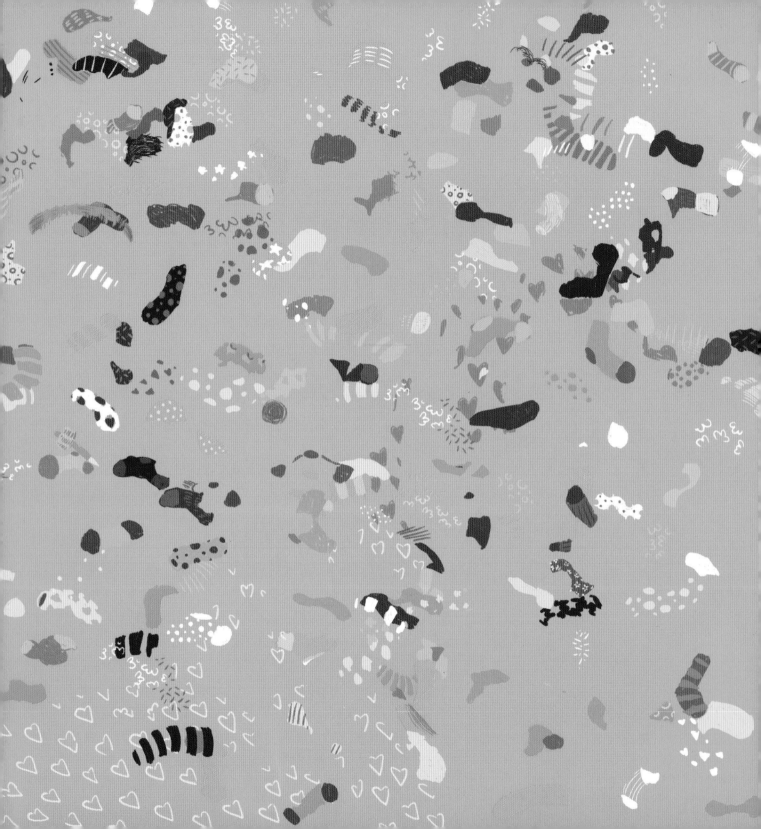

ברוך אתה ה׳ אלהינו מלך העולם שככה לו בעולמו

Dear G-d, Creator of the world, thank you for
making things just as they are.
– Blessing for the Wonders of Nature

Green Bean Books

First published in the Hebrew language in Israel in 2021 by M. Mizrahi Publishing House
First published in the UK in 2023 by Green Bean Books
c/o Pen & Sword Books Ltd
George House, Unit 12 & 13, Beevor Street, Off Pontefract Road, Barnsley, South Yorkshire S71 1HN
www.greenbeanbooks.com

Paperback edition ISBN 978-1-78438-947-5
Harold Grinspoon Foundation edition ISBN 978-1-78438-951-2

Designed by Ian Hughes
Edited by Michael Leventhal
Production by Hugh Allan

Printed in China by Leo Paper Products Ltd
1023/B2359/A5

FSC
www.fsc.org
MIX
Paper from
responsible sources
FSC® C020056

Just one more thing ...and then bedtime

Written and illustrated by Menahem Halberstadt

Translated by Romy Ronen

Green Bean Books

Dad!

What is it, Naomi?

I thought of something.

Just one more thing . . . and then bedtime!

It's so lucky that my ears can fold over a bit, because otherwise I couldn't squeeze t-shirts on.

That's very true.

And it's really good that I only have two legs,
because otherwise I'd have to find three socks
every day. And we'd have to get new pants.

True.
And now
it's bedtime.

It's lucky that Shabbat comes every seven days and we get to rest, because otherwise we'd be too tired to think straight.

That is true.

And it's lucky that my eyelids open and close, because otherwise sun would go into my eyes all the time.

Very lucky.
Now lights off!

And it's good that things fall down and not up,
because otherwise I'd have to climb up to get
my sandwiches and pencils off the ceiling.

And now, your head
should be down on
the pillow.

It's lucky that my nostrils don't point up,
because otherwise all the rain would
trickle inside, and I'd sneeze and sneeze.

Achooo!!!

It's nice that there are so many colors
in the world, because it means I can
draw butterflies, rainbows, and oceans.

Maybe I'll rest
here for a bit.

I thought of something else! It's lucky that there's more than one sound, because otherwise every song would be exactly the same.

Mmmm.

It's good the moon is so high in the sky because
if it were down here, we'd probably just stick
posters and signs all over it.

Mmmmm.

We're so lucky that we dream when we sleep. It would be so boring just waiting for the morning without dreams.

Right?

Dad?...

How lucky it is that we have cheeks,
because it's the best place for a goodnight
kiss . . .

Other books by
Menahem Halberstadt